Written by Gloria Patrick
Illustrated by Joan Hanson

THIS
IS...

CAROLRHODA BOOKS INC.
MINNEAPOLIS, MINNESOTA U.S.A.

Standard Book Number: 87614-003-7
Library of Congress Number: 70-84092

To Mike, Bobo, Kathy, Jesse
and all my other little ones

This is a mouse.

This is a house.

This is the mouse in the house.

This is a louse.

This is the louse
on the mouse
in the house.

This is a dog.

This is a log.

This is the dog on the log.

This is a bog.

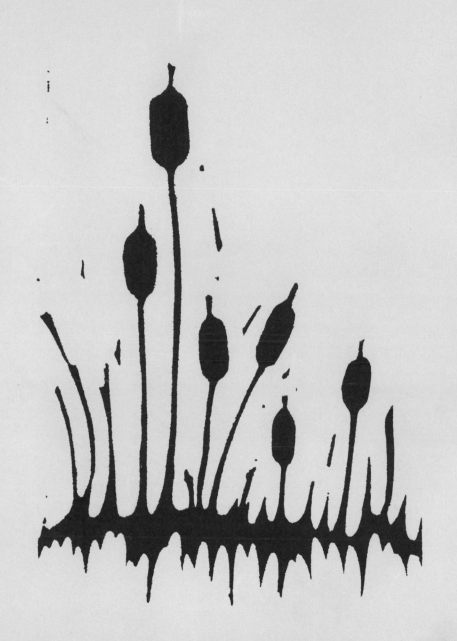

This is the dog
on the log
in the bog.

This is Jack.

This is a track.

This is Jack on the track.

This is a sack.

This is Jack
	with the sack
		on the track.

This is a jug.

This is a rug.

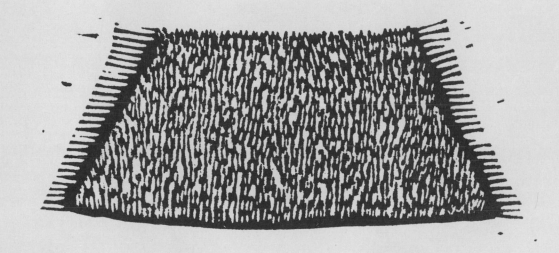

This is the jug on the rug.

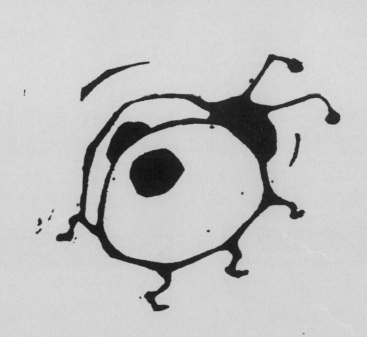

This is a bug.

This is the bug
in the jug
on the rug.

This is Kate.

This is her mate.

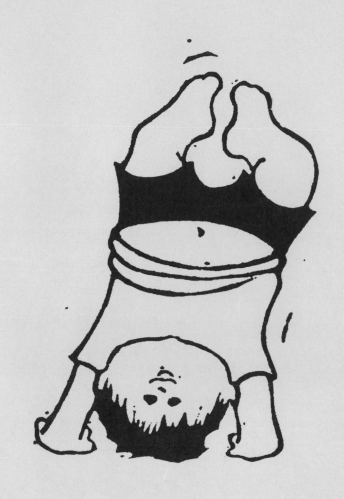

This is Kate and her mate.

This is a gate.

This is Kate
and her mate
at the gate.

This is a cat.

This is a hat.

This is the cat in the hat.

This is a mat.

This is the cat
in the hat
on the mat.

This is a bear.

This is a fair.

This is the bear at the fair.

This is a chair.

This is the bear
in the chair
at the fair.

This is a bee.

This is me.

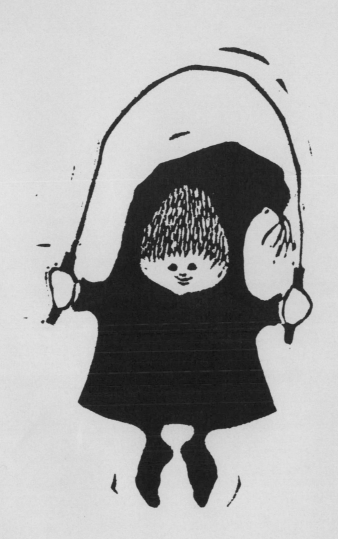

This is the bee chasing me.

This is a tree.

This is the bee
  chasing me
    up the tree.

This is a ewe.

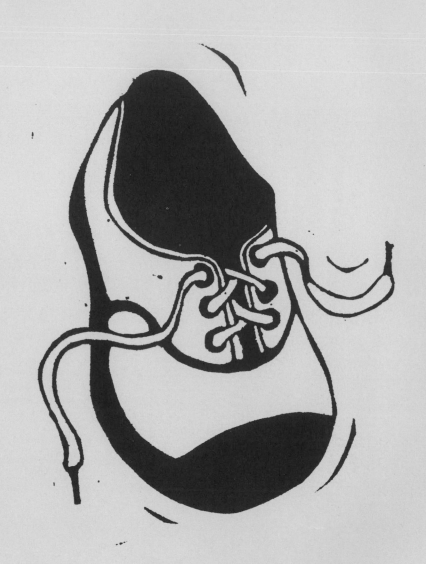

This is a shoe.

This is the ewe in the shoe.

This is a zoo.

This is the ewe
    in the shoe
        at the zoo.

This is my friend.